P9-BYY-758

DATE DUE

	PRINTED IN U.S.A.

56852

Manu-

factured in

Singapore

TWP 10 9 8 7 6 5

4 3 2 1

Library of Congress Catalog-

ing-in-Publication Data is on file.

ISBN 978-0-547-55863-9

The illustrations are drawn with pencil and
colored digitally. The text of this book is set
in Clichee.

www.hmhbooks.com

Houghton Mifflin Books for Children is an imprint of Houghton
Mifflin Harcourt Publishing Company.

For Santa, Mrs. Claus, and Dad, with love —D.U.

For Lynn, Ralph, and family (even Spice) —R.L

THE CHRISTMAS QUIET BOOK

By Deborah Underwood

Illustrated by Renata Liwska

Houghton Mifflin Books for Children
Houghton Mifflin Harcourt
Boston New York 2012

Christmas is a quiet time:

Mysterious bundles quiet

Searching for presents quiet

Getting caught quiet

Hoping for a snow day quiet

Bundled up quiet

Snow angel quiet

Knocking with mittens quiet

Cocoa quiet

Nutcracker quiet

Too tall tree quiet

Shattered ornament quiet

Star on top quiet

Lights on quiet

Blown fuse quiet

Gingerbread quiet

Gliding quiet

Someone's dad is a costume designer quiet

Forgotten line quiet

Helpful whisper quiet

Mistletoe quiet

Breathing clouds quiet

Luminaria quiet

Early Christmas gift quiet

Aunt Tillie's pickle and banana stuffing quiet

Reading by the fire quiet

Note to Santa quiet

Listening for sleigh bells quiet

Trying to stay awake quiet

Christmas morning quiet